Chapter 1

My name is TJ Barnes and I don't believe in ghosts — but my friend Seymour does.

Two weeks before Halloween, Seymour began acting strange. He asked if I could hear mysterious breathing when we were talking on the phone. He began taking "sneak peeks" into mirrors to glimpse something no one else could see. Finally, way too early in the morning, our doorbell rang. When I stumbled to the door, there was Seymour.

"Hey," he said and walked past me into the living room.

"Seymour," I groaned, "I'm not even awake yet."

"Sorry, but the world's greatest idea can't wait any longer," said Seymour. "Are your parents here?"

I shook my head. My parents took over the local hardware store last year. They work really hard at trying to make it a success, including going in early and staying late.

"Perfect," said Seymour. "They won't have messed up the evidence."

He was acting even stranger than usual. He was walking up to objects in our living room and just ... well ... peering at them. The remote control, *The World Atlas*, the lamp on the end table — he peered at them from above and then from below and then sideways.

"What on earth are you doing?" I asked.

Seymour looked at me meaningfully. He has short curly hair and crooked eyebrows, and his meaningful look was kind of lopsided. Or maybe it just seemed lopsided because half of my brain was still asleep.

"It's moved," he said.

"What's moved?"

"The atlas. Last night it was over on the bookshelf. This morning it's by the TV. Don't you wonder how it got here?"

"I know how it got here," I said. "There was a great TV show about diamond mines after you left. I was looking at maps of the north."

"Oh," said Seymour.

But Seymour is never stopped that easily.

"That lamp — you didn't move that lamp did you?"

"No," I said. "Seymour ... "

"Last night it was turned just slightly this way." He reached out and touched it very carefully with his fingertips. "Am I right or am I right?"

"I don't know," I said. "I don't care. I'm not even awake! What are you ... "

Seymour was halfway up the stairs, stepping on and off the fifth step. *Squeak. Squeak.* He looked around him as if the air itself was talking.

"Aha! Strange noises, moving objects. The place ... " he paused for

emphasis, "the place is haunted."

I was disgusted. Totally disgusted.

"Seymour! That step has always squeaked."

"Then the house has always been haunted — why didn't you tell me?" said Seymour.

"This is ridiculous." I climbed past him up the stairs. "I'm going to go back to bed. Wake me up at ten minutes after eight as usual."

"Seven minutes after eight," said Seymour, following me. "I always ring the doorbell at seven after eight. Any later than that and we'll be late for school; not that I really care if we're late."

He was peering at things again, the walls, the ceiling, down the hall. My best friend drives me nuts.

"You have to admit, this house has enough nooks, crannies and side rooms to be haunted," said Seymour. "How old is it, anyway?"

"It's not haunted," I said.

"But how old is it?" asked Seymour.

"It used to be my great-grandparents' house," I said.

"Then your gran would know how old it is," said Seymour. "We'll ask her when we go for the kittens today."

The moment he said those words, my whole world changed. A wonderful feeling spread through me from head to toe. The kittens! I'd been so mad at Seymour that I'd actually forgotten.

I'd been waiting for ages. Today was the day I was going to bring home Alaska and T-Rex.

Two months, that's how old kittens should be when they leave their mother. Seymour and I knew that because we'd done a report on cats last spring when I'd taken care of Gran's four adult cats. Those cats had almost driven me crazy, but I'd ended up liking them. Now I was going to take care of kittens of my very own.

"Do you want to see the food and water dishes I got for them?" I asked.

I take care of the pet supplies at the hardware store and I'd earned everything for the kittens myself.

"I saw them," said Seymour. "Five times."

"Did you see their new bed?" I asked.

"I saw the bed six times," said Seymour. He sighed. "But I could see it a couple more times. Maybe it's got a new piece of lint on it or … "

Seymour stopped dead in the hallway outside the spare room. He looked at me in that funny, cross-eyed way he gets when he's thinking hard about something.

"Now what?" I asked. I was almost willing to talk to him because I really had shown him the kitten bed at least six times already.

"Nothing," said Seymour, but he still stood there and he still looked cross-eyed. It was my turn to sigh.

"Go on. Tell me."

"There's a cold spot here."

"No big deal," I told him. "It's always cold right there. Even on a hot summer day or in the middle of winter when the furnace is blasting away, it's always cold by that door. It's just the spare room. There's some sort of draft or something."

"I don't feel a draft," said Seymour.

"It's just ... cold. Do you ever hear strange noises in this room? Knocking? Music?"

"Ghost noises, right?" I asked.

Seymour nodded.

"No," I said. "No noises. The house isn't haunted, Seymour. Why do you want it to be haunted?"

Seymour smiled and followed me into my bedroom.

"If it were haunted, our class could sell tickets to it on Halloween. And if we could sell tickets, we could make money. And if we could make money, we wouldn't have to sell stupid magazine subscriptions to go on our camping trip!"

At last things were beginning to make sense. Every year the kids in our grade go camping. Everyone looks forward to it, but we have to raise money by selling magazine subscriptions. I hate selling magazine subscriptions.

I looked at Seymour. I knew I had a decision to make and it wasn't an easy one. There's a reason I don't believe in ghosts. Ghosts scare me.

"Seymour," I said, "listen to me very carefully. This house isn't haunted. I don't want to live in a haunted house. It *is not* haunted."

"Okay," said Seymour. "I'm listening."

"But … " I said.

"But … " said Seymour.

"It *could* be haunted … " I said.

"Exactly … " said Seymour.

"If we turned it into a haunted house just for Halloween," I said.

"Hurrah!" said Seymour. "Let's go see if the kitten bed has magically changed color overnight."

Chapter 2

"Peeled grapes," called Amanda, waving her hand in the air. "I'll be in charge of the peeled grapes."

Seymour and I had told the teacher our haunted house idea first thing that morning. Ms. K. waited until just before lunch to discuss it with the rest of the class. She knows how easily our class gets off track. Ms. K. has taught us two years in a row.

"And spaghetti, I can do that too," called Amanda.

"We want a haunted house, not a food fair," complained Seymour.

"It's not for eating," said Amanda. "You blindfold people and tell them you have eyeballs in a bowl. If they're brave enough they reach into the bowl and feel … "

"Peeled grapes," said Seymour. He looked at Amanda with new appreciation. "Yuck!"

"And the cold spaghetti is worms," said Amanda. "If you want, we can put ketchup on the worms to make it look like blood when the blindfold comes off."

"Where did you learn this great stuff?" asked Seymour.

Amanda just smiled.

There were other ideas — lights that moved, eerie music, spooky decorations.

"Is everyone agreed?" asked Ms. K. "If I can get the school's permission, is this something we'd like to do as a class?"

Everyone's hand was raised.

"Thank goodness," said Ms. K. "I hate trying to sell magazine subscriptions."

Seymour and I arranged to meet Ms. K. at the hardware store later that afternoon. Before we got the school's permission, we needed my mom and dad to agree to turn our place into a haunted house.

"We'll clean up afterwards. We'll vacuum and wash the kitchen floor and tidy everything, even things we don't use," said Seymour.

"We'll put the hardware store on the posters as a sponsor," I explained. "It will be great advertising."

Mom and Dad had about fifty more questions, of course, but in the end they felt good about the idea.

"If it's helping the school and if it's going to be supervised, then I'm in favor of it," said my mom. She smiled and added, "Do you really wash floors, Seymour? Our house could use a good cleaning."

"I like the advertising idea. You're turning into a real businessperson, TJ," said my dad.

Actually, I'd just been trying to think of reasons why they should let com-

plete strangers wander through our house. Dad, however, was still smiling at me with his best "I'm proud of you, son" look. Parents who dream of having their own business and then manage to make it happen get really caught up in Hardware Store Land. They see everything as if they're looking out a display window.

Of course Ms. K. and my parents still had to talk the idea to death. By the time they were finished, Seymour and I were getting restless. The haunted house was a neat idea, but it was still two weeks off. Something else was a whole lot closer. KITTEN TIME!

Mom drove us over in the car. Gran was watching for us out the window. So were her four adult cats. It's a very strange feeling to walk up the front steps with five pairs of eyes following your every move. It could have been seven pairs of eyes, but T-Rex and Alaska were tumbling over and over each other in the middle of the rug.

Seymour and I had named the kittens ourselves. Seymour can't have cats

at his house because of his allergies, but he still likes them, and if he takes his medicine he's okay around them for a few hours. Seymour considers himself a dinosaur expert. He's the one who named the gray striped kitten with the white paddy paws after his favorite carnivore, T-Rex.

I'd named the calico kitten — all white and black and orange — myself. Her name was Alaska because her white fur was as bright and clean as new snow and because she had looked adventurous right from the start.

It was also her name because Gran's cats had used our redial button to phone Alaska thirty-seven times when they'd been at our house.

"I knew you'd be in a hurry," said Gran after she'd given each of us, including Seymour, a hug. "I've got everything ready."

I've always known my gran is the world's greatest grandmother, but she still surprised me. She'd built one of her carrying boxes for the kittens. It was painted with a prehistoric jungle

and an amazing assortment of dino-
saurs. The name *T-Rex* was painted
over the door.

"Wow!" I said. "Thanks!"

"I'll make Alaska her own box when
she's grown," said Gran. "They can ride
together for now."

"You're great at making things, Mrs.
Barnes," said Seymour. "Maybe you could
give us some pointers about fixing up
TJ's house."

My gran's eyebrows lifted.

"Our class is going to turn it into a
haunted house and charge admission
for Halloween," I explained as I tucked
the kittens one by one into the box.

"It's to raise money for their class
camping trip," said my mom.

I gave the kittens a last pat, told
them I'd take good care of them and
fastened the latch on the box. I looked
up just in time to see the look on Gran's
face. I can't explain why, but all of a
sudden I *knew* what she was going to
say next.

"Better be careful you don't wake
up the real ghost," she said.

I also knew what Seymour was going to say, but there wasn't anything mysterious about it. Seymour asks questions like water running downhill.

"What real ghost?" asked Seymour.

"The one in the spare room of course," said Gran.

My heart sank down to my toes.

Chapter 3

"Is there really a ghost? Have you seen it? What's it like? How long has it been there?"

They were Seymour's questions, not mine. I'd already heard way too much.

"Sorry, Seymour, we don't have time to give Gran the third degree," said my mom. "I have to get back to the store."

Once we were in the car, however, Seymour began asking Mom the same questions.

"Is it always in the spare room? Does it move around? Does it write messages

or knock on walls or cry at night?"

Mom just shook her head.

"This is the first I've heard of any ghost," answered Mom. "Gran lived in the house when she was a little girl, but after that it was rented out. We moved in three years ago."

"How old is the house?" asked Seymour.

"It was built in 1893," said my mom.

"Over a hundred years old! It's got to be haunted!" said Seymour.

I ignored Seymour as best I could. It wasn't hard. I was holding the box with Alaska and T-Rex on my lap. As soon as the car began moving they started mewing their little kitten hearts out. I opened the door and put my hand inside just so they'd know someone was still with them. After that they were quieter, but my hand felt weird because two small, rough tongues were licking it.

Mom dropped us at the house and then went back to the store. I took the kittens upstairs to show them the kitty litter. That was the number one stop

as far as I was concerned. Seymour stood in the cold spot outside the spare room.

"This is great," he said. "This really is a haunted house. We'll put it on the posters."

"No, we won't," I said. "Maybe it used to be haunted when Gran was little, but it isn't haunted any more. I know about these things. I live here."

After I showed them the kitty litter, I took the kittens into my bedroom and set them in the cat bed. They looked small and lost — two fluff balls with great big eyes. I was glad there were two of them. This was their first time away from their family and I would have felt sorry for them if they'd been alone.

Seymour settled cross-legged in the middle of the cold spot. From his position he could watch the kittens, but from the look on his face I could tell he was also thinking about ghost things.

That was fine. Seymour could think about ghost things if he had to. I was going to think about the kittens.

I sat on the floor beside them. That

seemed to make them feel better. Pretty soon Alaska crawled out of the cat bed and over my leg and began to look around the bedroom. She was the snoopier of the two. A little while later, T-Rex followed her. In spite of his name, he wasn't as brave unless his hunting instincts clicked in. We'd noticed that at Gran's house too. Just now he was happy to sit quietly as Alaska explored my bedroom, but when I shifted my running shoes under the dresser, T-Rex was after the moving laces like a shot.

Seymour laughed. The kittens were startled and then realized it was just Seymour. They peeked into the hallway. Alaska went first, of course, but T-Rex followed. When they reached Seymour they crawled over his legs, and Alaska began to climb her way up his back.

"Help," said Seymour.

Kittens have tiny claws, but they're really, really sharp. Seymour was making YEOWCH faces even though he was trying not to flail around and hurt either of them. I lifted Alaska from his back

and set her on the floor. T-Rex came over to check out what was happening. That's when they noticed the spare room.

It was weird how it happened. They just turned around and kind of froze in one spot. They sat down. They stared into the spare room.

"Hey," said Seymour. "Neat!"

"Neat what?" I asked.

"They're watching the ghost."

"No they're not," I said. "They're watching the curtains or the sunlight or the dust motes or something."

"Maybe," said Seymour. "Maybe not. Cats are sensitive to things — remember our report? Think about the way they warn people before an earthquake or find their way to places they've never been."

Seymour's eyes crossed with the effort of remembering.

"There was one story about a cat who jumped out of a living room chair every night after supper — just like it was being shooed out by its owner — except its owner had died months ago.

And there were lots of stories about cats visiting gravesites on their own."

Our cat report had had all sorts of facts about cats, and some ideas that may not have been easily proven facts but were interesting just the same. At least I'd thought they were interesting until now.

"No ghost," I said.

I picked up the kittens, one for each shoulder, and took them downstairs to show them their food dish.

That evening, Dad and I watched the kittens. We watched them investigate the "secret cave" beneath the china cabinet. We watched them pounce on dust balls. We watched them chase their tails. Kittens are just learning about the world. They do all sorts of goofy things adult cats are too dignified to think of doing.

Kittens also need someone to take care of them. Alaska took a great leap to a chair back, missed her hold and fell off backwards. I took my own great leap and caught her just before she landed in the fireplace.

"Good job, TJ!" smiled Dad. "You've

grown up a lot lately, and I don't just mean the cats. Do you realize that last spring you didn't even like the store and now you're taking care of the pet section and coming up with good advertising ideas? I'm thinking you could be even more involved. You could learn about different sides to the business."

He was looking at me with that weird "proud father" look again, but I didn't have time to think about it.

"Sure," I said automatically as I dove across the room just as T-Rex overturned the lamp.

By bedtime, the kittens were exhausted. That was good because I was exhausted too. They slept on my chest and moved up and down, up and down, every time I breathed. They weren't supposed to sleep on my chest, but what can you do when two little kittens start mewing because they miss their mother? They didn't weigh very much and their purring was neat. Kittens have big purring even though they're just little. I liked it.

At least I liked it until three o'clock

in the morning. At three o'clock in the morning T-Rex began licking my cheek — that rough little tongue again, and dinosaur hair in my nose. I set him back on my chest and lay there half-awake in the darkness. That's when I heard it.

Whooooooooooooooo. A hollow sound, a rushing sound.

Whoooooooooo coming from down the hall.

I craned my neck so I could see down the hall without leaving the safety of my bed. A glow was coming from the spare room.

Whoooooooo.

Don't look! Don't hear! Don't move!

That's what I told myself. There's nothing there. And even if there is something there, you don't want to know about it.

Whoooooooooo.

But I couldn't just lie there. My heart was going *wham, wham, wham*. My nerves were buzzing. I had to do something. The way I figured it, staying in bed and not knowing was scarier than

getting out of bed and finding out.

I set Alaska and T-Rex beside me on the covers and climbed slowly out of bed. The house was dark and quiet. All except for the sound. All except for the glow.

I crept down the hall. My heart was beating even faster. I got closer and closer to the spare room. I was at the cold spot now. A shiver went down my spine. I peered into the spare room. The window was glowing. *Whooooooooo.*

"TJ?"

I jumped about three feet in the air and spun around. In the half darkness I could just make out my mom peering around the corner. Her hair was wild and her eyes were skrinched up. Her voice sounded skrinched up too.

"Sorry, TJ. Did I scare you?"

Yes! Yes! Yes!

"Ahhh ... no," I said.

"What's wrong?" asked my mom. "Are you sick?"

Ghosts! Monsters! Werewolves!

"Ahhh ... I'm fine," I said. "I ... I heard something."

"What sort of something?"

I pointed towards the spare room.

"That sort of something," I said. "Whooooo."

Mom listened.

"It's the furnace," she said. "The air duct in the spare room comes straight up from the furnace and it always sounds twice as noisy at night when the house is quiet. Go back to bed."

Even as she spoke, the furnace shut off. By coincidence, the glowing at the window stopped as well. As soon as it stopped I knew what it had been all along. It hadn't been ghost-glow; it had been the motion light at the back of the house. All it took was a bit of wind moving the bushes to set it off.

The backdoor light, the furnace — everything had a perfectly normal explanation. I should have been relieved, but instead I was still feeling spooked. Darkness does that to me. I headed back towards my bedroom.

"TJ?"

This time I managed not to jump.

"How are the kittens?" called Mom

softly. "Do they like their bed?"

"Ahhh … sure," I said.

"That's good," said my mom. "It's best if they learn to sleep in their own bed right from the start."

I went back to my bedroom. I put the kittens in the cat bed. I climbed under my covers, picked up the cat bed and put it on top of my chest, kittens and all.

Prrrrrrrrrrr.

Safe at last.

Chapter 4

"But are you really, really sure it was the furnace?" asked Seymour the next day.

"I'm sure," I told him. "And I wouldn't have noticed it if you hadn't been babbling about cold spots and ghosts. No more ghost stuff."

I didn't tell him that after the furnace turned off I'd heard another sound — a whistling sound. It had also come from down the hall, but I didn't get up to see what it was. I'd been wrong about it being scarier to stay in bed. It was *way* scarier getting out of it.

"But Gran said there really was a ghost," said Seymour. "It won't go away just because you ignore it."

"Seymour!"

"I think you should ask your gran for the whole story, that's all. I mean, you don't believe in ghosts, so what's the harm in finding out the story?"

"I'll think about it," I said.

I thought about it through math. I thought about it through social studies.

"TJ, you don't need to be thinking about ghosts right now," said Ms. K. "Right now you need to be thinking about explorers."

I had my books open — how did she know I was thinking ghosts instead of explorers? As Seymour and I always say, Ms. K. is a witch ... not the nasty turn-kids-to-frogs kind, but the kind of witch that *knows* things.

When final period rolled around, Ms. K. announced that the principal had agreed to our idea for a haunted house. Now we could go ahead.

Gabe said his dad would donate some

dry ice so we could have mystery fog wafting around the entrance. Amanda suggested that Roddy could do some of his magic tricks and Jen, who's a real ham, could do scary stories with the old flashlight-under-the-chin trick. Other kids offered to help them out. Mia and her gang began planning decorations.

"Leave a place where we can hang some old sheets along one wall," said Amanda. "If we can figure out some way to hang them, we can hide behind the sheets and the walls can grab people as they go by."

Amanda really did have great ideas. Seymour was shifting back and forth in his seat, frowning harder and harder. I knew what was wrong. The haunted house had been his idea in the first place, and Seymour figured he should have most of the good ideas. That's the way Seymour thinks.

"At least let me tell everyone there's a real ghost," said Seymour after class.

I gave him my best *keep it quiet* look.

"We don't know there's a real ghost.

We haven't heard Gran's story," I told him.

"Then phone her and ask for her story," said Seymour.

"Seymour, I keep telling you. I don't want my house to be haunted. I have to live in it. Don't you understand at all?" I asked.

"Know your enemy," said Seymour. "That's what you told me when you dragged me to the library to find books about Gran's cats." Suddenly he got that cross-eyed thinking look on his face again. "Hey, that's a great idea. The library always puts out scary books for Halloween. Maybe I can get some ideas."

I wasn't sure the school library had the kind of scary books Seymour wanted, and I didn't want to watch him getting even more frustrated. I decided to head home. Amanda was going out the door at the same time.

"Where's Seymour?" she asked.

"He's looking for ghosts in the library," I said.

Right away, Amanda understood.

"I took over his haunted house idea,

didn't I?" she said. "I didn't mean to. I hope he thinks up some even better ideas just to top me."

She actually meant it. That's the trouble with Amanda: she's so nice you can't even get really mad at her.

"I didn't think you'd be this interested in a haunted house," I said.

Amanda shrugged.

"It's something different to think about, something fun instead of something ... " she sighed.

Amanda doesn't usually sigh. Amanda's the kind of person who is happy most of the time, another reason it's hard to dislike her. When she realized I was watching, she shrugged and brightened up.

"What about the sheets?" she asked. "Is there a place in your house we could hang them? It really scares people when the walls grab them."

"Let me think a minute," I said.

I wasn't really thinking about sheets; I was thinking about more important things.

I didn't want Seymour to feel that

I was teaming up with Amanda. That would make him even madder, and he was already pretty upset.

On the other hand, Seymour was right. I did need to ask Gran about her ghost story. In order to do that, however, I needed a little reassurance.

"Do you want to come over now and check out my house?" I asked.

Amanda looked surprised, but she nodded.

"That would be great," she said.

Right away I felt better. With Seymour going ghost crazy, Amanda's down-to-earth approach would help a lot. Amanda wanted to haunt the house, but she didn't think there were *real* ghosts.

"I'll have to go home first," she said, looking serious again. "I have to make a phone call."

"You can phone from my place," I said.

Amanda shook her head.

"It's better if I do it from home," she said. "I'll grab my bike. I can get to your place pretty fast if I take my bike."

The kittens were playing floor hockey with a milk bottle cap when she arrived — *scrabble, scrabble, scrabble, thwack* — across the wood floor of the entranceway. With the excitement of someone arriving, they did a couple of kitten explosions. T-Rex leapt for the sofa and did crazy jumps like an overhyped kangaroo all along the top. Alaska ran halfway up the living room curtains and hung there. I didn't know kittens could run straight up like that!

We both laughed. I climbed on the footstool to lift down Alaska. Amanda began looking around the house.

Our house isn't huge, but it does have lots of nooks and crannies. I think that's because it's been added to over the years. There are high ceilings, wooden arches and old-fashioned windows. There are stairs going up to the second story. There is even a small set of stairs going down to the kitchen at the back, which would make it easy for people to go through the place on Halloween.

"This is great, especially the way it's open beneath the stairs," said

Amanda. "We can hang the sheets from the railing and they'll fall right over this empty space. Kids can hide under here to do the grabbing and then they can knock on the steps when people climb up — double spooky. We can have cobwebs and neat stuff hanging from the high ceiling."

I showed her the upstairs.

"Mom and Dad's room is off limits, but we can use my room and we can do the eyeballs, worms and messy stuff in the bathroom."

Amanda had stopped in the middle of the hall by the spare room.

"Hey — this is strange," she said. "It feels cold here. Have you ever read any scary books? There's always a cold spot that sends chills up and down the reader's spine."

She turned and grinned at me.

"It looks like your house really is haunted after all!"

Wonderful.

Chapter 5

"I guess we should stop for today," said Dad, glancing at his watch. "The time sure flew by."

It was Saturday morning at the store. Dad and I were standing by the machine that mixes paint. Dad was looking at me with that "proud father" look on his face again. I was doing my best to be the intelligent and worthy son, but that's not how I was feeling. I was feeling confused.

"You can leave after you finish your pet section," said Dad. "You asked some good questions today, TJ. You're turning

into a real businessperson."

What questions? All I'd asked was why we put black pigment in the tin of white paint when in the end we wanted blue. I still didn't know the answer. Dad had shown me the paint chart as explanation, but the chart only explained what to do, not why to do it. And hadn't I heard that line about being a good businessperson before? What on earth was going on?

"You'll want to know these things one day," said Dad. He winked at me and headed off to help some customers.

I stared after him. For one brief flash, I thought I understood. Dad wanted me to take over the store one day.

My heart jumped up to my throat. I looked around me. The whole store. I might be the person to run it one day.

My heart crashed down to my toes. The whole store. I couldn't possibly run it — I'm just a kid! And I didn't even know if I wanted to run a store.

Don't think about it, I told myself.

Don't think about it. Adults are nuts. Adults are crazy, especially adults who run hardware stores. I had misunderstood something. It couldn't possibly be what was going on. There had to be some other explanation. And whatever it was would be completely crazy, so I shouldn't even try to figure it out.

I headed straight over to the pet supplies and began unpacking cat food like mad. That was good because it got me thinking about the kittens.

Alaska and T-Rex were still sleeping on my chest and waking me up with their rough little tongues, and I was still hearing noises in the house at night. Later today, when I was all alone in the house, I was going to lie on my bed with the kittens and listen to see if the house really did make the same noises in the day as it did at night.

When I finished the cat food, I unpacked leashes for dogs and cuttlebones for budgie birds. Taking care of cats had made me interested in all sorts of animals, and I liked learning about what people need to take care of their

pets. I filled up the shelves and wrote down things that needed ordering when the salesman came in on Thursday.

One of the order forms listed a book called *How to Train Your Cat.* I wondered if it had a section about kittens licking people in the middle of the night. I circled it to think about later, said a real quick good-bye to Mom and Dad and headed home.

Seymour was waiting on the steps. So much for the house being quiet this afternoon. He lifted a lumpy bag from the step beside him and followed me inside.

Mew, mew, mew.

We could hear the kittens as soon as we entered the house, but they weren't anywhere in sight.

"That's funny," I said. "They usually come to the door."

Mew, mew, mew.

Noises are strange things, even in the daytime. Sometimes you think you know where a noise is coming from, but as soon as you head in that direction you realize you're wrong. We

looked behind the sofa, in the kitchen, under the stacks of paper on the dining room table and then behind the sofa again.

Mew, mew, mew.

They were sounding more and more pathetic. Where were they?

"Found them!" called Seymour.

He was in the laundry room, peering into our tall, plastic, laundry hamper. The lid had slid in sideways. Sitting at the bottom of the hamper, mewing and mewing, were T-Rex and Alaska. They were too little to jump out.

"I bet the ghost dropped them in there," said Seymour. "Ghosts like to play tricks."

I frowned at Seymour and reached down to lift them out.

"No ghost," I said. "They've been climbing on everything in sight, even though they're not supposed to. They must have tipped the lid and slid inside with it. I found Alaska shut up in the cupboard under the sink this morning."

"That might have been the ghost too," said Seymour.

No ghost, I wanted to tell Seymour, no ghost. But hadn't I been planning on listening to the house this afternoon, just in case?

"Speaking of ghosts ... " said Seymour.

He fetched the bag from the front entry and set it on the kitchen table. Inside were library books. Some were from the school. Some were from the public library. Seymour was really determined this time.

"I've got good news and bad news," said Seymour. "The good news is — there are no such things as ghosts. It's all swamp gas or people's brains playing tricks on them or crooks taking advantage of people or magician's tricks. Here are the books to prove it."

He set a stack of books on the table. I looked at two of the titles.

Extra Sensory Deception

The Myth of Supernatural Science

"But here's the bad news," said Seymour. "Bad for you, that is — I think it's neat."

He plunked the second pile of books on the table.

"There really are ghosts. Here are the books to prove it."

This stack of books looked every bit as impressive as the first stack. The titles sounded every bit as official too.

The Science of Strange
True Ghost Stories

"I don't get it," I said.

"They're all in the same section of the library. Books saying there are ghosts. Books saying there aren't."

I didn't know what to say.

"But which are the true ones?" I asked.

Seymour shrugged.

"It depends on how you decide what 'proof' is. Or what it isn't."

I was getting more and more confused.

"Don't worry about it," said Seymour. "What we want right now are ways to haunt a house. There should be some great ideas here."

Seymour and I looked through the books. Actually, Seymour did most of the looking. I pretended I was helping,

but mostly I played with Alaska and T-Rex. It was fine for Seymour to get excited about ghosts; Seymour didn't have to live here. I was beginning to feel more and more like I was getting in way over my head.

"Weird smells ... that's something Amanda hasn't come up with yet," said Seymour. "TV channels that switch without anyone around; that won't exactly fool people because anyone can do it with a remote control, but it might add to the atmosphere if we switch from *Sound of Music* to *Curse of Dracula*. Billiard balls moving mysteriously on a pool table; that would be neat ... " He looked at me hopefully.

"No," I said. "My parents aren't going to buy a pool table just so you can figure out how to make the balls mysteriously move."

"Maybe I could move something in the kitchen then, like the toaster. I could do it with magnets."

It would have to be a huge magnet to move a toaster, but I didn't bother pointing that out. I was confused again.

"Are these things that real haunted houses have or things that pretend haunted houses have?"

"Real haunted houses, except if you believe this stack of books it's people's imagination or swamp gas or a big hoax and if you believe this stack of books it isn't. I explained all that already."

He read some more and sighed.

"None of these are dramatic enough," he said. "There was another book that the librarian couldn't find. Maybe it'll show up on Monday. Maybe the library has its own ghost that steals books."

After Seymour had gone, I began to look at the books myself. I only read little bits. I didn't want to get into the scary stuff. Basically, however, Seymour was right.

I read a paragraph from the "yes there are ghosts" pile.

And there, at the top of the steps, Megan Walters saw a figure in a long, flowing robe. Her small dog began barking — clearly the dog saw something as well. At that exact moment the neighbor across

the street, a respected doctor and com-
munity leader, looked out his window
and saw a figure in a long, flowing robe
standing on the Walters' doorstep. He
also saw it vanish into thin air.

I was sure there really were ghosts.
I looked at a book from the "no ghosts"
pile.

Although four people claimed to have
seen the "ghost," it was later discovered
that two of them had actually been away
from the house at the time and had only
seen a figure much later in the day when
it could have been almost anyone. The
third person, although present at the time,
was on a waiting list for cataract sur-
gery for severely blurred vision.

I was absolutely sure that ghosts
did not exist.
I tried another example.

As proof that Mr. Toft was commu-
nicating with a ghost, he provided de-
tails of childhood visits to the ocean as

well as the name and description of a much-loved dog. All of the information was accurate, although Mr. Toft had not previously known the family in any way.

Sounded like ghostly information to me.

I looked through another book.

A favorite trick for people pretending to talk to ghosts is to take a quick look into a family photo album while the client is distracted.

Did the mysterious Mr. Toft have a chance to look at a photo album? Would the ghostly figure seen by Megan Walters have been proven false if there had been a little more investigation?

I picked up a fifth book.

The scientific world once believed the world was flat and the sun revolved around the earth. Later science proved these "facts" were wrong. Is it not possible that the science of the future might prove ghosts truly exist?

And then in the very next paragraph ...

On the other hand, if you or I were to entirely make up a creature called a blimble and claim that science was not yet advanced enough to discover it ... would that mean our blimble creature was real?

All the books did was make me more and more confused. How could life do this to me? I'm just a kid. I need to know what's real and what isn't. I don't want to have to make up my own mind!

That's when the phone rang.

"Apple cobbler or chocolate brownies?"

Gran is like Seymour. She doesn't waste time with "hello, how are you."

"Hi, Gran!" I said. "The kittens miss you, but I'm taking good care of them."

"I knew you would," said Gran. "Cobbler or brownies?"

"Apple cobbler would be nice," I said. "Of course chocolate brownies are wonderful too."

"Some of each then," said Gran. "See you tomorrow."

Tomorrow? I got up and looked on

the calendar. Written on the square for tomorrow were the words *Special Sunday Supper.*

The good part was — Gran would be coming over.

The bad part was — we always sat around the table talking afterwards. Gran would be sure to ask about the haunted house plans and that would lead to the ghost story.

I took a deep breath and dialed the store to ask Mom if we could have extra company on Sunday. If the bad part was going to happen anyway, Seymour might as well be part of it.

Chapter 6

"Look!" I called. "The ghost!"

Seymour's head shot around. A paper bag was rattling its way towards us across the kitchen floor. It moved without strings, without wires and with a will all its own.

Suddenly a streak of gray flew from under the table to pounce on the bag. The bag exploded in a fluff of orange, black and white fur. Alaska and T-Rex rolled over and over on the floor in a joyous play-fight and then scampered off in search of more adventures. Seymour grinned.

"Alaska loves paper bags," I said, laughing.

"Are those kittens going wild again?" asked Mom, coming into the kitchen with a flower vase and a wrapped bundle of carnations.

"Just medium wild," I said.

"I wish they'd hold it down to medium wild on the back of the sofa," said Mom. "And the curtains in the spare room look like someone's been practicing Tarzan swings on them while we've been out."

She was smiling, but it wasn't quite a joke. The kittens were scratching and climbing more and more lately. Another thing I needed to train them not to do.

"They sure are cute little guys when they're not getting into trouble," said Dad.

Mom filled the vase with water and took the flowers into the dining room.

Everyone helped with Special Sunday Supper. Mom made bread and set the table. Dad cooked the main course. I was in charge of salad. Seymour had

come over early to help, so we decided to try something different — spinach salad with oranges, marshmallows and chocolate chips. It wasn't too bad if you picked out the marshmallows and chocolate chips and saved them for later.

Gran was pleased to see the kittens. She said they'd grown, even in the few days they'd been here. And, of course, she brought dessert. I'd made Seymour promise he wouldn't ask for the ghost story until the cobbler and brownies were served. I wanted to make sure I had dessert before I lost my appetite.

The moment it was set on the table, Seymour jumped right in.

"Anyone know a good ghost story?" he asked cheerfully.

I made my first helping a big one.

"Is that why you've been so quiet, Seymour?" asked Gran. "Have you been waiting to hear about the resident ghost?"

Seymour nodded.

"Actually there are two ghost stories about this house," said Gran.

"Is one of them about the bank robber

and his ghost stallion?" asked my dad.

Gran smiled at him.

"You tell it," she said.

"Are you sure? I don't want to steal it from you?"

"Go ahead," said Gran. "I enjoy hearing it from someone else. It helps me improve my timing."

I wasn't sure what that meant, but Dad seemed to understand. He set down his fork, leaned back and began to tell the story.

"A long, long time ago, back when people traveled by horseback, and cars were new and more than a little frightening, there was a bank robber around this area. His name was Wild Buck Mulligan. That was his name, wasn't it?" he asked Gran.

"Oh yes," said Gran. "He had a great black stallion, a wonderful fast horse he used for his getaways. He raised that horse from the time it was a colt, and that horse, wild as it was, loved Buck."

"Wild Buck and his wonderful black stallion robbed every bank in every town

west of here," continued Dad. "And one day they rode into town and robbed the bank on River Road."

"This River Road?" asked Seymour. "The one that runs past this house?"

Dad nodded.

"Wild Buck Mulligan and his black stallion went racing like the wind itself out of town, right past this very house. But just as they rounded the corner at the end of the street, a motorcar appeared. That stallion, wild and brave as it was, had never seen a motorcar. The horse was so terrified that it leaped into the air, throwing Mulligan to the ground. The fall broke Buck's neck and the stallion raced off, leaving Wild Buck dead on the street."

"Wow," said Seymour.

"The horse and the money were never found," said my dad, shaking his head.

"Never?" I asked.

"Never," said Dad. "And even now, late at night if the moon is full, you can still hear that horse racing past the house, looking for its long-dead master."

Dad turned to look out the window onto the street as if he might see the ghost horse. We couldn't help it. We all looked out at the street. And suddenly we heard it.

Tha-da-d-dup. Tha-da-d-dup. Tha-da-d-dup.

Seymour and I and even Mom jumped for a second. We looked at Dad. We looked at Gran. We looked at each other.

Tha-da-d-dup. Tha-da-d-dup. Tha-da-d-dup. We laughed. It was Dad, of course, drumming his fingers beneath the table to make it sound like the stallion galloping through the moonlight. We'd all figured it out at the same time.

"Good story," said Seymour, drumming his own fingers beneath the table. "I'll remember that one. Now tell us the real story."

Gran nodded. She finished the last of her pie. She took a sip of tea. Seymour watched her every move. My gran knows how to play an audience.

"Now then," she began. "When my parents first built this house, before I was born, they took in boarders. One

of them was an old gentleman who had spent his earlier years prospecting in the mountains."

"Diamond prospecting?" I asked.

Gran looked at me with sudden interest. Gran likes adventure shows almost as much as she likes having adventures herself.

"Did you watch that program on TV too?" she asked.

"It was neat," I nodded, "the way they found the sign of diamonds but no one believed them and they didn't even know where they came from."

"And so intriguing the way they tracked them all the way to the source," said Gran. "And then of course ... "

"Hold it, hold it," interrupted Seymour.

"Seymour!"

I glared at him. It's one thing to interrupt me, but it is not nice to interrupt my gran.

"Oops, sorry," said Seymour. "I guess I'm being rude."

"It's all right, Seymour. You want the ghost story, don't you?" said Gran.

"Please," he said. "If it's not too much

trouble. I mean, I can wait, I really can, kind of, but I have to be home by seven thirty."

I sighed.

"Where was I?" asked Gran.

"The old prospector," said Seymour.

"That's right. I think gold would have been the big find back then.

"Did he find any?" I asked.

"Some people did, but not Mr. Smithers," said Gran. "That was his name, I remember it now, Charlie Smithers. As I said, he was living in my parents' rooming house, so he must not have found the mother lode. He was a secretive old man and my mother had trouble talking to him at the best of times. Anyway, one morning when she went down to begin the breakfast chores, she met up with my father, who was coming in from the stable.

"'Abe,' she said, 'as soon as you get a chance, will you go up and see what Mr. Smithers wants.'

"My father looked at her in an odd way.

"'What do you mean?' he asked.

"'He's standing in his doorway, pointing up near the ceiling. He wants me to get something down for him, something above the window, but I can't figure out what it is. There's nothing hanging on that wall.'

"'Upstairs?' my father asked her.

"'Why yes,' she said.

"Once again my father looked puzzled.

"'Mary,' he said very gently, 'don't you remember? I took Mr. Smithers to the hospital last night.'

"'But you must have brought him back this morning,' said my mother.

"My father shook his head.

"'I was going to go after breakfast and check on him.'

"It was my mother's turn to be puzzled then. She went back upstairs. Charlie Smithers was nowhere to be found. She came down just as the clock chimed seven o'clock. They later found out that the old man had died that very morning, not ten minutes earlier, just at the time she had seen him standing in the hall upstairs."

"Wow," said Seymour.

"My mother said later that she probably dreamed it," said Gran.

"Except for the cold spot in the hall," said Seymour.

"Except for the cold spot in the hall," said Gran.

Brrrrrr.

Chapter 7

"It's a great story, but I don't think it's anything I can use," said Seymour.

I couldn't believe it. I'd finally been brave enough to listen to Gran's ghost story, and now Seymour was going to ignore it!

"I was awake all night because of that story!" I told him.

Seymour nodded his head sympathetically.

"Maybe you should ask your parents to move to a new house," he offered, "*after* Halloween of course."

"Seymour!"

"It's the same thing I told you before. It's not dramatic enough."

"Not dramatic enough?" I protested. "It's a ghost!"

"A ghost that hasn't been seen in eighty years except for a cold spot. A ghost that doesn't do anything," said Seymour. "Amanda has bowls of eyeballs and walls that grab people! Gabe has dry ice. Jen has spooky stories. And did you see what Mia brought this morning?"

I hated to admit it, but I could almost see his point. Mia had brought in a life-size skeleton. She promised it wasn't real bones, but her mother worked at the medical department of the university, so who really knew for sure?

As the week went on, all sorts of Halloween items were showing up at the back of our class — cobweb streamers, scary masks. One person brought in a black light and "glow in the dark" material that seemed to float in the air. We played eerie music during math, science and social studies so that we

could choose what we thought was the spookiest.

Between our classroom and Gran's scary ghost story, I wasn't sure if I was getting really excited or really worried about Halloween. Not to mention the fact that I had other things to worry about.

One of those things was the kittens. They were chewing everything in sight. Shoelaces were a favorite with T-Rex. I put on my running shoes, only to find the laces in three parts. I thought only puppies did that!

Alaska was climbing things like crazy — the living room sofa, the blinds in the kitchen. The curtains in the spare room had threads pulled out all along one side, like a set of railway tracks running halfway up. Why did she like the spare room so much? T-Rex had steered clear of it since the first day. Why hadn't Alaska?

I'd also found Alaska hanging halfway up the screen door. My parents weren't going to like the enlarged holes her little kitten claws had made.

And then there was my dad. He came into the bedroom while I was doing homework (or at least pretending to do homework — it's hard to do homework with a T-Rex chasing the end of your pencil) to ask me questions.

"Do you think we should put out the Thanksgiving stock right after Halloween?" he asked me. "Do you think it's better to advertise in the newspaper or on radio?"

I found a pamphlet titled *Small Business Basics* sitting next to my schoolbooks, and when I arrived at the store Thursday after school, Dad took me through the plumbing section.

Plumbing stuff isn't as interesting as pet supplies, or even as interesting as the paint machine, at least not to someone like me. I'm pretty sure it's interesting to plumbers because they work with it, but by the time we'd talked about valves and copper pipe and Y-drains, my brain was pretty well buzzed. Dad, however, was all enthusiasm.

"That's great, TJ," he said. "Next week we'll look at some of the electri-

cal stock together. You'll get to know the entire store."

I didn't know what to say. Was Dad really trying to teach me the business? I breathed a big sigh of relief when Seymour arrived.

"I've got it!"

Seymour's voice can be pretty loud anyplace, but it is especially loud indoors. He managed to rein in his excitement level for a moment, but once we hit the street it went up to about level ten again.

"I've got the book! It's great," said Seymour. "Guess what I'm going to do? I'm going to hold a séance!"

I knew what a séance was. A séance was when someone tried to communicate with ghosts, the way mysterious Mr. Toft had done.

"Seymour," I said right away, "this is a really, really, really bad idea."

"No it's not. It's a great idea. I'll have a table and there'll be knocking sounds and flickering lights and everything. I'll have my own sign — *Seymour Knows All, Seymour Sees All, Seymour*

Speaks with the Supernatural."

"No," I said. "No, no, no, NO!"

"But it's the idea I've been looking for," said Seymour.

"And it's the exact opposite of what I've been looking for. I want the ghost to go away, not come back!"

"What ghost?" asked Seymour. "You don't believe in ghosts, remember?"

"Seymour!"

"Anyway, this isn't about real ghosts," said Seymour. "This is a book about tricks. One story is about how Harry Houdini showed that things done at a séance could be done by simple magician's tricks. The secrets are in the book. And they're easy."

Harry Houdini was a famous magician. I really admired Harry Houdini. Now I was actually listening.

"Picture this," said Seymour. "You come into the room. It's all darkness except for one little lamp in the corner throwing shadows on the wall. There's a crystal ball on the table. I get you seated and look mysterious and peer into my crystal ball."

He peered into his hands and lowered his eyebrows.

"I see that you are worried about someone close to you … "

He looked at me expectantly.

"Did I tell you about my dad acting weird?" I asked.

Seymour smiled and shook his head.

"But you've noticed it, right?" I asked.

"Nope," he said.

"I don't get it," I said. "How did you know?"

Seymour grinned.

"You told me yourself. All I said was that I see you are worried, and you told me the rest. Think about it," said Seymour. "If you walked up to anyone, especially an adult, and said 'You're worried about someone close to you,' wouldn't it almost always be true?"

I thought about it. My mom was always worried about my gran, my dad and me. My dad was always worried about my mom worrying too much. My gran was pretty good at not worrying about people, but she certainly worried about her cats.

"They're called Barnum and Bailey statements because they're like a tricky circus act. They're statements that suit almost everyone," said Seymour. "The book explains how not to be too obvious. I'll have to work on that. But here's another good one ... "

Again Seymour peered into his hands. Again he lowered his eyebrows.

"I see you lost something, something that you were very sad to lose."

Instantly I felt a chill down my backbone. When I'd been babysitting Gran's four cats, I'd lost one of them. It had been really awful until Seymour and I had found her again.

Seymour and I! Suddenly I came to my senses.

"You knew about that!" I said.

"About what?" asked Seymour.

"About me losing Cleo. You were there!" I said.

Seymour smiled and nodded.

"But think about it," he said. "Wouldn't it work anyway? You must have lost something I didn't know about."

I thought about it. It was such a

little thing that I didn't mention it to anyone, but last summer I'd lost my favorite rock. It had a neat stripe on it and it fit into my pocket like an old friend. Thinking about it made me miss it all over again.

Seymour was right. What person in the world hasn't lost something they didn't want to lose?

"Hmmmm," I said.

"So a séance is a great idea!" said Seymour. "You don't have to be spooked about it. It's not ghosts; it's psychology and circus tricks. At least that's what my séance is."

I looked at Seymour. He had that very, very hopeful look he has on his face when something really matters to him.

"You have to say you're a fortune-teller, not a medium," I told him.

"Okay," he said. "Not many kids know what a medium is anyway."

"And don't use the spare room. You can use my bedroom," I said.

Even if he wasn't calling himself a medium, I didn't want him in the spare room.

"Your bedroom is full of cat hair," said Seymour.

"It'll add to the atmosphere. Cats and magic go together, remember?" I told him.

Seymour had one of his abrupt changes of opinion.

"Good idea," said Seymour. "The kittens can stay in the room with me. It'll be nice and quiet and they won't get lost with people tramping in and out of the house."

Now that was a good idea.

"Maybe I can teach them to help me levitate the table," said Seymour.

I didn't know what to say to that one, so I said nothing at all.

Chapter 8

"Onions," said Gran.

"I thought onions were supposed to scare off vampires," I said.

"Garlic for vampires and colds. Onions for cats. You could try it," said Gran.

I'd phoned her about the cats shredding the furniture. I wasn't sure which Mom would like better — strings hanging from the material on the sofa or bags of onions draped across it.

"And a scratching post of course," added Gran.

Talk about missing the obvious. Maybe I could get the kittens to stop

scratching up the place after all.

"What did you think of the ghost story the other night?" asked Gran.

"Pretty scary," I admitted.

"I hope it isn't giving you nightmares," said Gran.

"Not exactly," I said.

Of course "not exactly" didn't fool Gran.

"You know, TJ, it's a good story, but even my mother said that it probably *was* just a dream," said Gran.

"Why would she dream something like that?" I asked. "Why would she dream about Charlie Smithers standing in the hall, pointing into the room or whatever?"

"He was very, very sick," said Gran. "My mother would have been wondering if there were relatives that needed to be told. Her dream could have been her way of figuring out that, secretive as he had always been, in this case it would be okay to go through his private papers. Maybe he would even want her to go through them. Haven't you ever had that type of dream?"

When Gran's cat Cleo was lost, I dreamed that I found her under the neighbor's steps. She wasn't there, but my mind *had* been trying to work things out in my dreams.

"Did she go into his room?" I asked. "She must have, afterwards I mean."

"Yes, she did, but she never found anything personal — papers or letters or anything to tell much about him. A mystery man — that's why it makes a good story — although it did puzzle her. She was sure she'd seen him writing in a journal at one time or another."

Gran sounded thoughtful.

"But you see what I mean, don't you? She'd been thinking about him. It wouldn't be surprising that she would dream about him."

That night I felt a little better when I went to bed. At least I felt better for a while.

Scrabble, scrabble, scrabble.

Three in the morning.

Dark.

Quiet.

Scrabble, scrabble, scrabble.

I hate noises at three in the morning. Noises at three in the morning drive me nuts. Especially when I live in a house with a ghost story.

I reached for the kittens on my chest. One kitten ... T-Rex from the shortness of its fur. Two ... Two ... No two kitten! Where was Alaska?

A cold trickle of sweat ran down my neck. I couldn't help it. By daylight it's easy to ignore Seymour and his "the ghost did it" theories, but at three in the morning the whole world changes. I had to find Alaska.

I picked up T-Rex and set him on the covers. I climbed out of bed. I snuck down the hall.

Slowly.

Quietly.

Why was I moving slowly and quietly? If it was a ghost, didn't I want to scare it away? But that's not how my brain thinks at three in the morning. At three in the morning all my brain can think is, don't let it know I'm here, don't let it know I'm here.

Slowly.

Quietly.

Scrabble, scrabble, scrabble.

The sound was coming from the worst place it could possibly be coming from. It was coming from the spare room.

Scrabble, scrabble, scrabble — thwack!

It was the *thwack* that gave it away. Suddenly I felt a whole lot braver. All I needed was a little light.

I reached into the spare room. I turned on the light.

Thwack!

I stood dazed for a moment. Gradually, my eyes adjusted. Yup, I was right. Alaska was standing in the middle of the room. She blinked at me, leaped into the air, danced sideways, pawed something on the floor in her crazy sideways shuffle and sent it skidding towards me.

Thwack — it hit the baseboard.

Hurrah! No ghost! Just a hockey-playing cat!

I bent to pick up the hockey puck. It was small and round and golden. A ring. I turned it slowly in my hand. Carved on it was a pair of initials.

Don't look. Don't look. Don't look.

I didn't look. I picked up Alaska. I went back to my bedroom. I climbed under my covers and put the kittens on top. I held the ring tightly in my hand beneath the covers.

Only when daylight returned did I look at the initials. I was glad I waited. I wouldn't have wanted to find out the answer at three in the morning.

C.S. — Charlie Smithers.

Chapter 9

The thing I don't get about life is the way little things start piling up until suddenly there's a great big heap and it's hard to separate one thing from the other, except you begin to feel like you're on the bottom somehow.

First, the ring — our house really was haunted.

Second, the kittens — Mom and Dad had found the holes in the screen door. And the loose threads on the kitchen blinds. And the chewed corners on the T-bone steak. And the shoelaces in pieces. And T-Rex with butter on his whisk-

ers. And Alaska playing hockey with my mom's favorite earrings. And the tracks up the spare room curtains.

And third was my dad. I found a sheet of paper in the stockroom. He'd been doodling on it. *Barnes' Hardware* he'd written. That was okay. That's the name of our store. It's not very imaginative, but it works. Below that, however, all outlined in bold lines as if it were a sign or letterhead or something official, was more writing. *Hardware Haven — Barnes and Son.*

I was right. He expected me to run the business. I should be feeling proud! I should be feeling great! Instead I felt sick inside. What was wrong with me?

"You don't look very well, TJ. You'd better go home."

Mom actually left the store's checkout counter to put her hand on my forehead. That's how lousy I was looking.

Home wasn't where I wanted to be either. The ghost was at home. What other explanation could there be for the ring showing up in the middle of the floor at midnight? I hadn't told Mom

or Dad or even Gran and Seymour about it. I knew I'd have to tell them sometime, but it's hard to explain. Sometimes there are things you have to figure out on your own before you go blabbing about them.

"Is it okay if I drop by Seymour's house just for a few minutes?" I asked. "There's something he wants to show me."

"Okay," said Mom. "But take it easy. You don't want to be sick for Tuesday."

Tuesday was Halloween.

Three days away.

"It's great, isn't it?"

Seymour had found a real crystal ball at a garage sale. It was round and smooth and wonderfully clear. It seemed to bend the light inward and reflect it all at once. No wonder people thought crystal balls were magical.

Seymour had fixed up a portable dimmer switch that he could work with his toe to make the lights flicker. He had also found a toy with a plastic squeeze

ball that opened the lid on a garbage can so a monster could pop out. He was working on a way to use it to make the card table lift at his bidding.

"You don't need my help," I told him. "You're doing just fine on your own."

"I am, aren't I," grinned Seymour. "Besides, you're already late for Amanda. I told her to sit on your front steps after lunch and you'd show up eventually."

Sure enough, when I got home, Amanda was waiting. She had a bundle of sheets for the haunted house. We hung them over the bottom of the stair rails. They were going to work perfectly.

"Can you store them somewhere, so I don't have to carry them back on Tuesday?" Amanda asked.

We took them upstairs and I put them in my bedroom on the safe side of the house. That's how I'd begun to think about the upstairs — the safe side and the haunted side. When I came out of the bedroom, Amanda was over on the haunted side, standing in the

cold spot. She was actually smiling.

"Do you know what this reminds me of?" she asked.

"You already told me," I grimaced. "Scary stories."

"Not this time," she said. "This time it reminds me of my grandpa's truck."

That's another thing about Amanda. She doesn't usually say what you think she's going to say.

"I don't get it," I said.

"When we go out to the farm, sometimes I sit in my grandpa's old truck. It makes me feel close to him, even though he died a few years ago."

"But ... is there a cold spot? Aren't you afraid of his ghost or something?"

"No cold spot," Amanda smiled. "Even if there was, it wouldn't matter. My grandpa wouldn't hurt me. In fact, I don't really understand why anyone thinks a ghost would hurt people. I mean, I like scary stories as much as anyone, but I like them because they're stories. Your mind can make you think as many good things as bad things, I guess."

Amanda amazes me. Some of the

books I'd been reading had hinted at the same thing, even though they dressed it up in all sorts of ways. That's when I asked her something I probably shouldn't have. I don't really know Amanda well enough to ask her personal questions.

"Is that why you're so sad sometimes? Because of your grandfather?"

Amanda stepped out of the cold spot.

"No. I miss him, but it's a different kind of sad," she said. "It was quite a few years ago."

She scooped up T-Rex to give him a kitten cuddle.

"Do you promise you won't tell? I don't want people to start asking me about it."

I nodded.

"My little cousin is sick," said Amanda. "She has to have special treatments. She's going to be okay, but she's just a little kid. Little kids shouldn't have to go through stuff like that." She sighed again. "I phone her and tell her jokes, but I wish there was something else I could do."

"I'm sorry," I said.

"So am I," said Amanda.

We stood there for a while longer, not saying anything at all. Sometimes it's okay not to say anything at all. Alaska broke the silence.

Mew, mew, mew.

It had to be Alaska because Amanda was still cuddling T-Rex.

Mew, mew, mew.

The sound was coming from the spare room. Oh no, I thought, not again. I felt cold right down to my toes, but I knew I couldn't just ignore it. When you decide to take care of kittens, you have to look after them, ghost or no ghost.

Amanda and I looked inside the spare room. We couldn't see Alaska, but the sound was louder.

Mew, mew, mew.

Strangely enough, it seemed to be coming from behind the wall, high up where the curtains bordered the top of the window. The words from Gran's story came back to me.

"He's standing in his doorway, pointing

up near the ceiling ... above the window ... "

That's when I noticed that the path of plucked threads now went all the way up to the top of the curtains.

Mew, mew, mew.

"Where is she?" asked Amanda.

"I don't know for sure, but I'm going to find out," I said.

In the end, I had to stand on two pillows on top of a chair on top of a table in order to get high enough to rescue her. There was a ledge above the window, and behind it, built in such a way that it would only be found if you knew what you were looking for or had the sound of a lost kitten to guide you, was a small opening.

I reached into the opening and down into the wall below. Right away, something rough began licking my hand.

"She's in here," I said. "There's a bunch of other stuff in here too."

I pulled out Alaska and handed her down to Amanda. I reached back inside the opening. I brought out a metal box, something soft wrapped in oilcloth

and two dull-colored rocks.

And that's when I began to come up with a great idea of my own.

Chapter 10

"Ahhhhhh!"

The scream was terrifying. It shrilled through the house. It made my blood curdle. And it made me laugh. It was coming from Ms. K.

"Oh," she said, recovering herself with a gasp. "You're right. This is way too scary for little kids."

Our haunted house was about to open. We were testing it on Ms. K. The walls had just grabbed her. Her scream confirmed that the haunted living room, the stairwell and the upstairs room with *Seymour the Haunted Fortune-Teller* would

only be for older kids. The little kids could come into the kitchen for regular magic tricks, bobbing for apples and scary stories depending on how brave they were feeling. Ms. K. would be there with her witch's outfit to be a little scary but not too much.

Ms. K. climbed the stairs. Seymour ushered her into his haunted, fortune-telling room.

"You are worried about someone in your family. I see palm trees, wild winds and stormy seas," he said.

Ms. K. looked at him.

"How did you know that, Seymour?"

Seymour looked mysterious for a moment. Then he grinned and turned back to regular Seymour again. After all, this was Ms. K. Ms. K.'s powers of observation far exceed our own.

"You told us last year that your sister was moving to Florida," said Seymour. "And this year you're teaching us a lot about hurricanes. I put the two ideas together. I learned to do things like that from you. You're a good teacher."

"Thank you," said Ms. K. "I think."

She walked down the hall. We'd put a large white paper circle on the floor where the cold spot was, and I'd hung a sign on the door of the spare room.

Ghost in Residence. Enter if You Dare.

"What's this?" asked Ms. K. "Is this the project you were talking about, TJ?"

Before I could answer, the doorbell rang. Our first guests had arrived.

It didn't take long for the screams and giggles to start, about an equal number of each. Everyone had a good time.

Amanda was in charge of taking money. The box was so stuffed with bills she had to give some to Ms. K. for safekeeping. We did great business for about two hours and then it began to slow down. Just before eight thirty I heard Amanda call.

"TJ — they're here!"

That meant Mom and Dad were driving up. We'd given them a special invitation. Neither Seymour nor I had told them the details about what our class was going to do to the house, just so we could surprise them. I had

a surprise all my own; that's why I stayed upstairs, but I crept to the landing so I could hear Amanda talking down below.

"Front door or back?" she asked.

"What's the difference?" asked Dad.

"The front is the scariest, but it costs more," said Amanda, "except it's free to you because you live here."

They chose the front door and insisted on paying. They said they'd be able to make a better judgment on whether or not they got their money's worth that way.

The front hall was dark and spooky. Eerie music played and jack-o-lanterns grinned.

The living room was full of cobwebs and tombstones. Rats poked in and out of the curtains and crawled over the sofa. They were plastic, but in the dark they looked real. A bat swung across the room, brushing Mom's hair. Mom screamed. Someone raced out from behind a tombstone, shouted "Boo!" and disappeared. Mom screamed again.

"TJ!" she called. "You didn't tell me it was going to be this scary!"

I didn't answer, but I could see her from the top of the stairs. Seymour and I were chuckling. Dad was laughing. He hadn't been scared yet. He walked by the stairwell. The sheets grabbed him. He jumped about two feet. It was Mom's turn to laugh.

Up the stairs ... *knock ... knock ... knock.*

Seymour hurried off to wait for them in the séance room.

"Come in, come in," he called. "Let Seymour the Amazing tell your past, your present, your future."

Mom and Dad were in the séance room for at least ten minutes — I think Seymour gave them the special treatment. Next they visited the creepy bathroom.

"From now on, whenever I climb in our tub I'll think of eyeballs," said Dad.

"I still want to know how Seymour knew I'd lost my glasses," said Mom.

They stopped in the paper circle to feel the cold spot.

"This was a good idea, using what's already here," said Mom.

"I've tried and tried to figure out why this spot is cold and fix it, but I have never been able to," said Dad. He pointed at the sign on the spare room door. "What's that?"

"*Ghost in Residence. Enter if You Dare,*" read Mom.

"Shall we?"

"I don't know if my heart's up to it," said Mom.

"We'll be sorry if we don't," said Dad.

Very, very slowly, Mom opened the door of the spare room. Very, very slowly ...

"Hey!" said Mom

"Neat!" said Dad.

The spare room wasn't dark and spooky as they might have expected, but it had been changed from the way it usually was. A scratchy old blanket, a canvas rucksack and some work clothes lay across the bed. A pickaxe, shovel and the type of wide, shallow pan that prospectors use to pan for gold were leaning against the opposite wall. On top of the dresser were rock samples — quartz, lead, limestone,

sandstone and fools'gold. Beside them were maps with mining claims marked on them. All those things, if Mom and Dad had looked closely, were things they would have seen somewhere else — our basement, Gran's garage, Seymour's attic.

But what lay on the desk was something they hadn't seen. It was a small book with a leather cover, yellowed pages and flowing writing.

"The room's done up like a prospector's cabin," said Dad. "And this looks like a journal or diary."

"Do you see the name?" asked Mom. "I don't believe it — Charlie Smithers."

"That's the name on this photograph too," said Dad. It was an old-fashioned photograph, a tintype. The man in the image had sharp, questioning eyes, a handlebar moustache and a huge floppy hat.

At that moment Charlie himself rose up from behind the desk — moustache, hat and all.

"TJ?" asked Mom.

"Rats," I said. "I was hoping to fool you for a few minutes anyway."

Chapter 11

Enough money to go camping in the mountains twice — that's how much money we made from the haunted house.

Seymour was really pleased.

"It was my idea you know," he said. "I'm probably a marketing genius or something and I don't even know it!"

"But we don't need to go camping twice," said Gabe. "Maybe we could buy a thousand bags of candy just to get us through the year."

Ms. K. didn't bother to answer that one.

"We could give the money to help kids who couldn't come to the haunted house or even go out for Halloween,"

I suggested. "Kids who have to stay in the hospital or visit it a lot."

"There's an organization that does special events for kids like that," offered Roddy. "We could give the money to them."

That's what we decided to do.

"Thanks, TJ," said Amanda after school. I just nodded. I was glad I'd thought of it. Amanda turned to Seymour as he came out the door. "Thanks for the fun, Seymour. The haunted house really was a great idea."

"Are you going to tell me where you got all the neat scary ideas?" asked Seymour.

"My grandfather used to do those things on Halloween," said Amanda. "Every year when we went to his house there'd be something special set up. It got scarier the older we got. It was great. He was a real character."

Those were about the same words Mom and Dad used when we talked about Charlie Smithers after supper that evening.

"I still can't believe he fixed up a hiding space in the wall above the window

and no one knew about it," said Mom. "If Alaska wasn't so snoopy it might have been another hundred years before anyone found Mr. Smithers' journal, if ever. Maybe a little kitten wildness isn't so bad after all."

"The journal and the photograph," said Dad. "You can guess just from the look in his eyes what an interesting character he must have been."

"Have you read very much of the journal, TJ?" asked Mom.

"I'm working on it," I said. "I've been trying to follow Charlie's travels on the maps Gran brought over. It's really neat to see where he went and what areas are actually being mined today — copper, magnesium, coal. I'm trying to find out what those two rocks he kept might be."

"I didn't know you were interested in that sort of thing, TJ," said Dad.

What happened next is kind of hard to explain. I scooped up the kittens and set them in my lap and started talking to them. The words just kept pouring out.

"I'm interested in all sorts of things," I said. "I'm interested in cats and dogs and pets and maybe veterinarians and animal training and circus acts. I'm interested in gold mines and diamond mines and all sorts of minerals and old photographs. I'm interested in how to prove whether or not there are ghosts or even if you *can* prove them or disprove them. I'm interested in more things than I even know about. I might even be interested in hardware stores and paint and advertising and business, but how can I know what I'm really interested in until I get there because there's so much along the way? I mean, I might even turn out to be a character myself."

A great silence followed. I was looking at the kittens. Dad was looking at me. Mom was looking at both of us.

"Is there something going on here that I don't know about?" she asked softly.

"I guess there is," said Dad.

He sighed. It was a big sigh. I looked up. He was shaking his head. And then

he smiled. It wasn't the hardware store dad that was smiling either. It was the real dad, the one that's there underneath, only sometimes I worry he isn't there even though I should know he really is.

"I guess I went a little overboard about teaching you things," said the real dad. "I guess I forgot that running a business is our dream, not yours."

I got even more worried then. I didn't want Dad to misunderstand or Mom either.

"It's not that I don't think it's neat," I told them. "It's just that I don't know what I want to be when I grow up. I mean, I don't even know if I *could* do what you do."

"Oh you *could* do it, TJ," said my dad, "but you don't *have* to. You really don't. I mean that. And if I ever forget, I want you to jump in and remind me again."

I nodded. I especially liked the "jump in and remind me" part. I know what hardware store parents are like. I could see something weird happening again

in the future, but at least now I felt like I might have some way out.

"Why don't you just be TJ Barnes for now," said Mom. "You're pretty good at it."

"Pretty good," said Dad. "But if you're going to be an independent character like Charlie Smithers, you should probably find out the scientific reason why we put black pigment into white paint in order to make it blue because I don't understand it no matter what the charts say."

He really did understand ... at least sort of!

I put Alaska on one shoulder and T-Rex on the other shoulder and went upstairs and stood in the cold spot.

Some of the mysteries of life aren't really so mysterious — Seymour and his séance showed me that.

On the other hand, there are things in life that aren't easy to explain.

I'll never know whether the figure that my great-grandmother saw was real or dreamed. I'll never know whether I found the journal because a ghost

wanted me to or because a kitten was a little too adventurous.

All I know is that someone I've never met, a prospector named Charlie Smithers, feels like a friend of mine.

Maybe, just maybe, I believe in ghosts ... some types of ghosts ... after all.

Seymour's bag of books held the following titles.

Broughton, Richard S., PhD. *Parapsychology: The Controversial Science*. New York: Random House, 1991.

Fraser, Sylvia. *The Book of Strange*. Toronto: Doubleday, 1992.

Gardner, Robert. *What's So Super about the Supernatural?* Brookfield: Twenty-First Century Books, 1998.

Gordon, Henry. *Extra Sensory Deception*. Toronto: Macmillan, 1988.

Inglis, Kim and Tony Whitehorn, Editors. *Ghosts and Hauntings*. New York: Readers Digest, 1993.

O'Neil, Terry and Stacey L. Tipp, Editors. *Paranormal Phenomena: Opposing Viewpoints Series*. San Diego: Greenhaven Press, 1990.

Smith, Barbara. *Ghost Stories of Alberta*. Willowdale: Hounslow Press, 1993.

Hazel Hutchins has always loved ghosts. She is the author of many beloved books for children of all ages. A master storyteller, Hazel weaves together humor, suspense and characters who live on the page. *TJ and the Haunted House* is Hazel's second book for Orca Book Publishers. Her first, *TJ and the Cats*, is shortlisted for the 2003 Silver Birch Young Readers' Choice Award and is on the 2002 list of Best Books from the Canadian Toy Testing Council.

Hazel lives and writes in Canmore, Alberta.

Praise for *TJ and the Cats*:

"Charmingly written and genuinely funny in a gentle, sophisticated way, this is a delightful short novel for readers ages 7 to 11."   *Quill & Quire*

"Hutchins' wonderful lilting style is refreshing and enjoyable. Highly recommended."
Resource Links

TJ and the Cats
1-55143-205-6
$6.95 CAN; $4.99 US
paperback, 108 pages

To family and friends.

HH

National Library of Canada Cataloguing in Publication Data
Hutchins, H.J. (Hazel J.)

TJ and the haunted house / Hazel Hutchins.

"An Orca Young Reader"

ISBN 1-55143-262-5

1. Haunted houses — Juvenile fiction. I. Title.

PS8565.U826T32   2003   jC813'.54   C2002-911438-1

PZ7.H96162Tj   2003

Library of Congress Control Number: 2002115989

Summary: TJ worries that he has taken on more than he can handle when he agrees to turn his home into a haunted house to raise money for a school trip.

Free teachers' guide available.

Orca Book Publishers gratefully acknowledges the support of its publishing programs provided by the following agencies: the Department of Canadian Heritage, the Canada Council for the Arts, and the British Columbia Arts Council.

Cover design by Christine Toller
Cover & interior illustrations by Kyrsten Brooker

Printed and bound in Canada

IN CANADA	IN THE UNITED STATES
Orca Book Publishers	Orca Book Publishers
1030 North Park Street	PO Box 468
Victoria, BC Canada	Custer, WA USA
V8T 1C6	98240-0468

05 04 • 5 4 3

TJ and the Haunted House

Hazel Hutchins

ORCA BOOK PUBLISHERS